VIOLET
BENT BACKWARDS
OVER THE GRASS

Lana Del Rey

獻給每個疲憊的人，
午後溫暖的雙手偶然碰上這扉頁——
不管你在哪兒邂逅——也許你會想起，
這世界在幫助你，
而你也用同樣的姿態回應。

Violet bEnt bAckwards Over The gRass

薇奧菈在草地嬉戲

薇奧拉在草地嬉戲

我去了一個派對
聲勢如雷
下了幾個決定
毫無動搖
會讓我開心的事
該做還是不做
靜靜斟酌每個選項
縝密計畫細思慢想

但我走進大門
穿過開放空間
看見了薇奧拉
　　　　在草地上嬉戲
七歲的她手裡
　　　　緊抓著蒲公英
倒立弓身像座橋
如狂人般咧嘴笑
滿溢無所事事才能迸發的活力
等待著煙火綻放的絢麗

就在那一瞬間
我決定無所事事地面對所有事

永遠。

赤腳踩著地氈

希薇雅‧普拉斯啊　請走好妳的路
別像一個個跌落的那些人們

別把情人和母親的祕密帶進妳的孤墳

那些妳藏著的祕密會讓妳身不由己　一如父親兄長和艾咪[1]
妳在街上遭遇的每個人　都會重複著她的謊言

讓我自己靜靜　我央求
深夜坐上一艘小船漂向卡塔麗娜沒有理由

微微汗珠點綴我額頭
在攝影季可能像晨露

唉　但這人生真實得很——要我的思緒停止背叛只有困難
一個探問的理由？
因為她跟鎮民說我瘋了他們就開始相信謊言

但不管怎樣——我已經繼續前進

既然我已將那一切都焚毀[2]
我疑惑下次落腳會在何方
是惡火稍歇的索諾馬
還是南第科達？

當我站在總統山下　真的會有美國人凱旋歸來的感覺嗎？
那一切
那偌大雕像的宏偉真能取代我從沒擁入的溫暖懷抱嗎？

還是我就該活在當下
在廚房裡
赤腳踩著地氈
無聊——但沒有不開心
在沸水上切切菜　待會就成了燉菜

註：
1. 應是指Sylvia的爸爸、哥哥，還有她崇尚的詩人Amy Lowell，其因女同性戀身分受到議論。
2. 此段雙關加州的森林大火事件。

離開你之後的事

完美花瓣點綴藍黃絨呢
房間散落裝滿草莓的銀色盤子

穿涼鞋在Zimmerman[1]挑夏日洋裝

三個女孩
白眼連翻
放聲大笑
午後塵埃都被點燃

我的人生甜如檸檬飲如今不再有苦澀果實
刪除記憶迎向陽光
不再想起你

我的思緒大轉彎
歌聲比從前高亢
已凌駕在你之上

沒有光點閃爍於我腦海中的電影
在貝爾維放映

因我擒拿了心滿意足
就航向仙納度[2]

一波波襲來的憂傷我掌舵穩住

乘著內心未熄的火順風飛向馬里布

此刻一切已完美
我有本錢能虛度

幾朵完美花瓣
幾張綠色刺繡椅
等我挑件夏日洋裝

註：
1. 澳洲女裝名牌，正確拼法為Zimmermann
2. Xanadu，墨西哥度假勝地

LA，我哪有資格愛你？

LA，我名不見經傳哪有資格愛你
LA，我身無分文哪有資格愛你
在我心亂如麻的當下
我沒什麼能夠給你

LA
不全是座永不闔眼的城
不全是座清醒的城
卻完全是座作夢的城
如果你把夢魘都當作夢

LA
我是個作夢的人
但我名不見經傳 哪有資格作夢

LA
我很沮喪！
我想發牢騷！
請聽我說
他們說我為錢而來 但我沒有 我甚至沒有愛人 這不公平

LA
我用生活權換了張鉅額支票
可如今我徹夜難眠原因費解
加上我超愛Saks[1]所以我究竟為何而來
明知道我無法久留

LA
我看上了舊金山 因為那個不愛我的人在那

LA！
我好悲慘
但你也一樣
我可以回家了嗎？
無親無故的孤兒
單人座位
無人熟識的Delilah[2]千人派對
我前夫在那裡上班
我受夠了這一切
但是

我可以回家了嗎？
無子無女的母親
一個人搭私人飛機
回去那棟藏著千檔殺人詭計的都鐸洋房
Hancock Park[3]待我不善我懷恨在心

註：
1. Saks Fifth Avenue 薩克斯第五大道，紐約奢侈品連鎖百貨公司。
2. 洛杉磯的高級餐酒館。
3. 洛杉磯高級住宅區旁的公園，附近有都鐸和義大利復興風的老屋。

街角的女巫
沒人想要的鄰居
讓市長大人多聘了幾位保全

LA！
我知道我錯了 但我無處可去 我可以回家了嗎？
我從來就沒有母親
你願不願意讓我占有豔陽
把大海當作我兒
儘管我是孤兒 我仍擅長照顧東西
我可以認養你的山嗎？
我發誓會讓她們更加翠綠 把她們當成女兒
教她們躲開各種水深火熱

我很寂寞，LA
我可以回家了嗎？

我為了舊金山離開我的城市
我在金門大橋上寫作卻事與願違
一位富翁免費載了我一程而我也帶上了我的
打字機 也對自己發誓會留下來
但
事情跟我想的都不一樣
不是我自己感覺的不一樣
是冷是暖也都沒關係

只是我不屬於任何人，所以
我只有一個地方能待
那座不怎麼清醒的城
那座不怎麼熟睡的城
那座還能是什麼的城──不上不下
那座還在抉擇
它好壞的城

噢還有

我沒你睡不著

沒人像你一樣摟過我
擁抱得不深
但我感受到你在我身邊
在我身邊抽著菸
在我身邊輕輕抽著菸
我好喜歡你喜歡霓虹燈
就像我一樣
橘色的
遠遠的。我們都很愛而我喜歡我們
這麼像

且我們都回不去紐約
對你來說，是靜止的。
對我來說，到死前都不屬於那座城。
操他媽的紐約郵報！

LAAAAA！
我哪有資格需要你 因我需要的太多
要求的太多
你給了我什麼我仍不確定 我可能到死還是不確定。

現在
我知道的是我配不上你
不是最棒的你，當那些挺拔的尤加利樹在我的國度裡壯觀擺盪
不是最糟的你──
燃著熊熊大火，住不下人也無法呼吸。
我一點也配不上你
你看看──你有母親
有塊大陸棚
你誕生之處還有一大片沃土

而我是個孤兒
擱淺在你原生岸上的小小貝殼
當然我只是眾多貝殼中的一個 但正因如此
我別無選擇只能愛你比任何人都還多。

因為這樣──
請讓我愛你
別在意我的迫不得已
讓我抱緊你 不只為了假期 而是真真切切直到永遠
讓這一切成真，讓我當你真正的妻子
女友、情人、母親、好友。
我仰慕你
別對我拙劣的言詞興趣缺缺
我平常都靜靜靜靜的，儼然是冥想者
其實我到尤迦南達[1]靈修中心就會表現優異 我很確定。
我保證你幾乎不會看見我
除非你想看見我
除非你偏愛一個愛哭鬧的小孩
如果真是這樣我也可以打開開關！
我在舞臺上技藝非凡你可能知道，你可能聽說過我？

註：
1. Paramahansa Yogananda(1893-1952)在美瑜伽導師。

聽過沒聽過我都會適應得好好的
所以什麼也別做就這樣愛我
或許除了別變動你的疆界
我是你的 如果你願意
放聲宣告或竊竊私語
誠摯的 你的女兒
無論如何
你是我的。

i measure time by the days i've spent away from you
that thought occurred to me
as i watched the sky go dark from blue

我用離開你的天數來計時
突然有了這個想法
當下天空從灰黯變成了湛藍

千火之國

兩班藍色鐵製列車疾急駛過你沁涼如鐵的深邃藍眼睛
弗農
採石場[1]
這廣袤讓我美麗的心靈空空淨淨
狄倫
注視你的那刻我聽見「狄倫」
在我的手臂上看見這兩個字就像隱形墨水刺青
那陰和我的陽兩兩相對
剛勁配上了我的柔弱無邊
就是男子氣概的最好證明
自顧自地筆直毫無動搖
對峙著所有元素
光明與黑暗
就像太陽溫暖著我凋萎的花蕊
就像土壤滋養著野花不在意她生長何處

弗農
這裡的一切都著火了
誰都無法倖免於難
灼熱的空氣正在燃燒
我從沒真的熱戀
但不管這感覺如何形容
我希望每個人都身歷其中
這地方像一個人
熟悉
像某個曾站在我身畔的人
但不像曾站在我身畔的你
謝謝
你在這裡
把我的廣袤都親眼目擊

這些年我曾喚你出沒我的航道之間
瘋狂狀態的你
是構成我的世界的那顆衛星
模仿著我內心不願承認的混亂
重播著我上半輩子的懲罰
映照著我的憂傷

若我要繼續用現在的樣子活下去
我就不能沒有你
我的雙腳搆不著土地
需要你的身體才能站立
你的名字才能把我定義
作為一個女人
我很恐懼
和
飄逸
以及

我的雙眸中有七個世界

我能同時身在其中

有個世界住著我的繆思醞釀著我的詞
另個世界在木星的右手邊 夜深人靜時我很努力駕馭
當然還有我生活的這個世界
千火之國
你大駕光臨的入口

你
弗農
狄倫
兩班藍色鐵製列車
疾急駛過你沁涼如鐵
的深邃藍眼睛

帶我遠離年少
我看得模模糊糊的世界
引我航向高聳的海崖
在漫長的公路上

航向未來之地
一個我陌生的世界
充滿滴水的花朵和超現實
在過於偌大的太陽系中

你　弗農　狄倫

不必隻字片語吸去
黑暗的夜
無須解釋我雙眼中的星球
在工廠的燈光下肩併著肩
讓我能做我從前的樣子
如果一切都能有美好結局

3 種不一樣的結局
流過我薄冰上的血液
我飛黃騰達因為我說我願意
因為我寫了我願意

但其實如果你不在這裡
我不知道一切能否如昔

所以不管我在哪個世界
都靠衛星為自己導航
弗農
狄倫
和瘋狂狀態的你

兩班列車疾急
駛過你沁涼如鐵的藍眼睛

註：
1. 應是火車站名。

不去天堂（草稿）

願我的視線總是平行地面
願我的雙眼永不望向天堂
去試探原因
那些原因我發現在此生
無足輕重 遠不如當下的美好
而這是許多難題的解方

~~願我永不涉足 天使害怕觸足之地~~ 因此不少
對空中的答案
無動於衷

不存在任何理由
如果有，算我頭上
但至少我不會花一輩子等待
在晨曦中搜索神的存在
側耳傾聽另個世界的聲音
在300億光年之外

不 這事我會讓別人去費心
他們費心之際我會躺在庭院草皮
開著電視讀些無關緊要的書

我會義無反顧地早起當然——
只為了幫你泡杯咖啡

Joe 我今天早上想著——
就是像這樣的時光
我倆從愛店的窗
一起欣賞海霧緩緩上騰
我祈禱我的視線永遠平行你的雙眼
永不下沉墜落到桌布之間
當時太緊張不敢分享心底的聲音
和你

Joe 你知道
就是像這樣的片刻 海霧緩緩上騰
我倆站在碼頭上 伴著燭光
我開始偷偷地想
有些事還沒告訴你
像有時我害怕自己的悲傷太難癒
有天你可能得幫我一把
但到時再說吧——

願我的雙眼總是望著天際線
打量映著金光的那排新宅
矗立於長灘海岸之外
不去天堂

因為我對人類有信仰 不管這聽起來有多怪
至少在那些片刻與時光之中
這不只是因為 我在你棕色眼眸中覓得的溫暖
是因為我相信自己的善良
足夠讓你種下一桿旗幟
或一朵玫瑰
或一段嶄新的生命

不去天堂

願我的視線總是平行地面
願我的雙眼永不望向天堂
去試探原因
願我永不企及 天使害怕駐足之地
因此不必 對空中的答案急急尋覓
那些原因我發現在此生
無足輕重 遠不如當下的美好——
是許多難題的解方
不存在任何理由
如果有——算我頭上
但至少我不會花一輩子等待
在晨曦中搜索神的存在
側耳傾聽另個世界的聲音
在300億光年之外
不 這事我會讓別人去費心
他們費心之際我會躺在庭院草皮
開著電視讀些無關緊要的書
我會義無反顧地早起當然——
只為了幫你泡杯咖啡
Joe 我今天早上想著——
就是像這樣的時光
我倆從愛店的窗
一起欣賞海霧緩緩上騰
我祈禱我的視線永遠平行你的雙眼
永不下沉墜落到桌布之間
Joe 你知道
就是像這樣的片刻 海霧緩緩上騰
我倆站在碼頭上 伴著燭光
我開始偷偷地想
有些事還沒告訴你
像有時我害怕自己的悲傷太難癒
有天你可能得幫我一把

但到時再說吧
願我的雙眼總是望著天際線
打量映著金光的那排新宅
矗立於長灘海岸之外
不去天堂或來生
因為我對人類有信仰 不管聽起來有多怪
至少在那些片刻與時光之中
這不只是因為 我在你棕色眼眸中覓得的溫暖
是因為我相信自己的善良
足夠讓你種下一桿旗幟
或一朵
玫瑰
或一段嶄新的生命。

德莎・迪比特麗

每個碰過我的都想殺了我
除了第六街和Ridgeley轉角的治療師

那位名字已被我忘記的女巫
隨口推薦了德莎・迪比特麗

她說我最大的問題 是磁場讓人難信任
我問她該怎麼辦 她頓了一下說
沒辦法
隨即讓我無法自拔泣不成聲
對那些重要的事 你總是束手無策

她說
好吧，有個方法可以試試
想像地板正在上升要撐起妳
再沉入妳身後的床腳下
太多能量蓄積在妳的前方和上方

讓我想到之前看過的一場演唱會
吉姆・莫里森 在好萊塢的露天劇場
1968?（待查證）
棚架上的藍色燈光給他一種靈氣
彷彿被光暈包圍——讓他貌似有八呎或更高
當時只覺他靈魂已出竅
像極了站在舞臺上的神

所以我告訴她
也許藝術家真得要活得有點出神
若他們真想傳遞天上的旨意

她接著說
專注如一是傳遞的關鍵
妳該盡力發展內在直覺
閉上眼睛感受妳的注意力核心
若在眼窩後頭就慢慢推到心臟中央
讓那裡成為妳思緒匯集的地方
不少人這麼做就能未卜先知

噢——然後吉姆27歲猝逝
所以如果你想在歌詞中找天堂 就去看看別人的歌
你讀過「人類很奇怪」的歌詞嗎？
他不是個合理的存在。

灌木叢後柏樹鬱鬱蒼蒼

我在鏡中看見妳
髮型和從前不同
身邊的空氣也不同
妳說想長髮中分
貌似寂寞了許久──他有別的女人讓妳憔悴

長灘

漫無目的

妳手指一揮就擦去了紙上的油　準確
堅決一如藝術家看不見卻有種視野

用一個理由
挾著怨恨瞪向天花板
而非草皮
雙眼直直
望向了地平線
準確
如雷射般的視線

時間慢了下來
穿越妳的存在
那些推動妳的一切
指揮著妳

　　不思不想地移動著

與緩緩下沉的太陽相覷
在刺眼的午後時分
沐浴在夏日傍晚的火熱
像隻鳳凰像飛機尾像沒人收聽的廣播波段

喬治雅　歐姬芙
喬治雅　蜜桃姬
心無旁騖地畫著妳的畫
永永遠遠
忘了教妳的老師
原諒他離開妳

愛在滋長
無法抗拒
臉頰泛紅
是你駕到

現在道別
　無可避免
過好人生
　就像沒人聽見

成為生命呼吸的藝術
成為世界運轉的靈魂

盡其在妳
只為自己
不必付出
只顧攫取
反正沒人聽見

萊姆路和第十街的盡頭碧綠又蜿蜒
　　　　　灌木叢後柏樹鬱鬱蒼蒼越過鐵絲網
　踩緊油門
　　　　　開上更遠更人跡罕至的路
　妳在那兒揭開運動休閒衫
我終能看清妳的真面目

站在那鬱鬱寡歡幽幽沉沉
雙眼不藍但清澈宛如
天堂

妳不想被忘記

妳只想消失而去

運動輕型機

在我33歲生日那天我去上了飛行課沒有打給你 也沒有把車停在我們舊居的街區
傑納西
傑納西
傑納西
我知道這樣有點悲哀，但我有時還是喜歡把車停在那裡 在車裡吃著午餐 覺得好像離你近了一些
我曾愛上這裡的一切
和你 在那間小公寓裡
樹頂的黃色小花是我們望向窗外的唯一風景──足夠讓我看見我們的未來。
但最後 只剩我一個人看得見了。
蠢斃了的單身公寓。爛透的你。讓我等著的你
你
你
你
像一張壞掉的唱片無限跳針

所以生日那天我覺得有些事該改變，不能總是等著你

別告訴任何人 但
我去上飛行課的理由之一 是想成為自己的領航者──天空中的大隊長 也許這樣我就不必再從你身上 尋找方向。

然後，這個一時衝動的想法意外地展開。當時不好意思跟對方說我的第一堂課就是最後一堂。我只好每週去報到。在聖莫妮卡和邦迪｢罕見的小小機場上。
我們從體驗迴旋和滾轉開始 一切都很順利。但沒過多久就出了狀況──
在我天空中的第四堂課，我的教練──
比我年輕但健壯如你──教我一些基本操作
我沒有不聽指令卻非常猶疑 緩慢地傾斜運動輕型機 向右上轉彎。
害怕。我害怕自己會控制不了飛機
教練一點都不客氣也不溫柔地搖了搖頭
看也不看我就說：「你不信任你自己。」
我嚇壞了。覺得自己不知怎地被看穿。

就像他認識的我──懦弱得無可救藥

當然他只是在說我開飛機的技術。但我知道自己會把那句話聽得很深。它對我來說有更深的含義。
我不信任我自己。

不只是在馬里布海邊2500英尺上空
而是隨時隨地。然後我也不信任你。
我當時可以說些什麼卻沉默不語
因為飛行員不像詩人
他們不會在天空和性命之間恣意比喻

在這些充滿自我審視擊垮信心的中年駕駛練習之間，我也決定試試一直想做的另一件事——在生氣蓬勃的瑪麗安德芮灣上學開船。我用伊莉莎白・格蘭特的名字報名沒人眨一下眼睛。我很確定當我走進 Bali Way[2] 狹小的棚屋時有人會說：「你不是船長也不是天空的主人。」沒錯，但漁夫們不會在意我也不會。

在這個短暫的瞬間我覺得比以前都還更像自己，

讓那位自稱是船長的醉漢教我的字字句句洗滌我 就像海面上的泡沫。

課才上到一半，我額頭就開始發燙 雙手轉帆到紅腫，船長告訴我在海上最重要的一件事。絕不要把船撞進鐵裡頭。

那是個航行的術語 意思是不要逆風行船。你要知道風從哪裡來才能避免這個錯誤。而你可能沒有時間抬頭看桅杆或更遠處的風標

所以你要感受風從哪裡來——

透過你的臉頰，透過白色的浪尖——

透過它們起落的方向。

於是他給了我一道練習。

他要我閉上眼睛，用脖子感受風從哪邊來。我有種預感自己一定會答錯。

於是我告訴他

「風從四面八方來——我覺得它無所不在。」

「錯了，」他說。「風是從左邊來。從港口那一邊。」

我坐等他跟我說：「你不信任你自己。」

但他默默無語，我就開口幫他說。

「我不信任我自己。」

他大笑出聲，比飛行教練溫柔卻渾然不覺那道練習題的挫敗傷我至深。

「這和妳信不信任自己沒關係。」他說。「就只是因為妳不是船長。妳不靠這行吃飯。」

他要我每天練習 讓我慢慢進步。

「妳都去哪家大賣場？」他問我

「帕里薩迪的 Ralphs。」我回應。

「好。那下次你去帕里薩迪的 Ralphs——我要妳——從停好車到走進店門的那段路——閉上眼睛感覺風從哪裡來。我沒有要妳像個瘋子蹲在停車場正中央但不管妳去哪——我都要妳試著感受風從哪裡來 然後判斷它是從港邊還是右舷吹來 這樣妳回到船上時就更能掌握了。」

我覺得他的建議很可愛。我已能想像自己在停車場瞇眼的樣子 一旁的主婦看得目不轉睛。我能想像自己漸漸掌握風從哪裡來 同時一點一滴的信任也在我的內心滋長。

註：

1. Bundy Drive，Santa Monica 的一小徑。

2. 港邊小路之一。

我想過把這些都說出來但還是默不作聲。
因為船長不像詩人
他們不會在大海和天空之間恣意比喻
在我這麼想的同時
我發現──
這就是我寫作的原因

繞地球一周的這些航程
都讓我慢慢返回人生
再去個月球6趟 讓我的詩意升騰
我不是個船長
我不是飛行員
我在寫詩
我在寫詩。

LA. Im from nowhere who am I to love you
LA. Ive got nothing who am I to love you
when Im feeling this way
and Ive got nothing to offer

LA
not quite the city that never sleeps
not quite the city that wakes
But the city that dreams for sure
If by dreams you mean nightmares.

LA
Im a dreamer but
Im from nowhere who am I to dream
⟨LA Who am I to Love You⟩

沉默的服務生—永遠的藍（草稿）

甜美的小寶貝服務生 你的移動行雲流水
你不屑討好任何人 卻讓整個夜晚微笑
在午夜安靜地做著木工 我們待會見
我的愛我的笑我的保護和造物主
我對你的感覺有點像痛楚
我腹中的宇宙在燃燒
懸在半空搖搖欲墜
星球的排列獨特無比
我身體裡的地球環繞著太陽
全是海洋不見陸地

水世界
追日者
南回歸線
南半球
我是隻哭泣的甲殼動物
在鈔票裡晒著日光浴
月球。
讓我們重寫一次這最初悸動的氤氳
可以嗎親愛的？
如果我說這一年讓我覺得
我們可以寫得比他更好
是否有點厚顏？(和月球 押韻？)

但我何德何能 紙上作夢
只是個愛在日記塗寫的女孩
默默安排好的詞彙
與你相戀 最
我的藍色 沉默的服務生
~~永遠~~
夏日
~~沉默的服務生~~
或是 藍色 永遠？
下班記得打給我
我等等就把你接回 / 夜越深就越完美

夜越深越好

正確版
與你相戀
我的藍色 永遠
夏日 沉默的服務生
下班記得打給我
越晚就越完美
越晚就越完美？

下班記得打給我
越晚就越完美 ?
越晚就越完美

與你相戀
我沉默的服務生
夏日
藍色 永遠
下班記得打
等等我
我等等就把你接回
夜越深就越完美

甜美的小寶貝服務生你的移動行雲流水
你不屑討好任何人卻讓整個夜晚微笑
在午夜安靜地做著木工我們待會見
我的愛我的笑我的保護和造物主
我對你的感覺有點像痛楚
我腹中的宇宙在燃燒
懸在半空搖搖欲墜
星球的排列獨特無比
我身體裡的地球環繞著太陽
全是海洋不見陸地
水世界
追日者
南回歸線
南半球
我是隻哭泣的甲殼動物
在鈔票裡晒著日光浴
月球。
讓我們重寫一次這最初悸動的氤氳
可以嗎親愛的
如果我說這一年讓我覺得
我們可以寫得比他更好
是否有點厚顏？
但我何德何能
只是個愛在紙上作夢的女孩
默默安排最好的詞彙
與你相戀
我沉默的服務生
夏日
藍色
永遠
下班記得打給我
我等等就把你接回
夜越深就越完美
凌晨十二點零五分
夜越深就越完美

因為我的臥室現在是個神聖境地／有孩子們在床腳
跟我說故事

去年我寫給你最後一封信
（我未來詩集創作的開始）
我第一次把你的真面目看清
我從沒用別的名字喚過你
我想讓你知道 你的真性情我早已知曉──
讓我見證邪惡
提醒我黑暗確實存在
告訴我惡魔就在眼前
告訴我怪物常看不清自己的真面目

但投射真是件有趣的事
你放火燒完了房子
還想說服我 說我才是拿著火柴的那個人
你說 我不知道自己幹了什麼好事
你說 我不知道自己的真面目

但我的確知道自己的真面目。

我喜歡玫瑰園
每次有人離開我 我都會買些紫羅蘭
我喜歡優勝美地高大的紅衫
如果妳要我的姐妹說 想到我時萌生的第一個念頭
她會說
木頭燃燒時的煙霧

我喝醉時
很溫柔
也很有趣
雖然我上次喝醉是14年前

我常跟很多朋友去海邊 他們不知道我的瘋癲
我可以去海邊
我可以做任何事──
包括離開你

因為我的臥室現在是個神聖境地
有孩子們在床腳
跟我說故事　說他們會假裝討厭一些朋友　隔天再跟他們和好──
有剛採的鮮花　由我自己栽種
在Big Sur老友送的他親手雕刻床頭櫃上的花瓶裡
我待在這裡越久，自己就越確定
我越認真寫詩　就越少陷入有你的思緒
我越認真寫詩　就越少陷入有你的思緒
　　　　　　　　我越認真寫
　　　　　　　　詩　就越少陷入
有你的思緒
　　　　　我越認真寫詩　就越少
　　陷入有你的
　　　　　　　思緒
我
　　越
　　　　認真寫詩
就越少陷入
床上
有
　　你。

在班尼迪峽谷的丘陵中

在班尼迪峽谷的丘陵中　愛能恣意滋長
我的打字機綠燈正燦亮
距離我上個男人已有兩個月時間
鄰居的空地上不再有雙屍命案在醞釀
我靜靜望著暮色，還足夠星光巴士航行。我聽著嬉痞對山腳下的貝菈小徑無意義囔囔
猛踩油門掠過雪倫道和生命的崇高
我仔細傾聽
謝謝免費載我一程
謝謝提醒我一切都會變成故事
提醒我要是能笑就別哭。

但後來我找不到落淚的理由
至少不在今晚的七點二十七分
數月以來我第一次覺得靠近天空
在班尼迪峽谷的丘陵中
電視聲化成的背景音樂裡
愛能恣意滋長。
沒有祕密沒有理由去推遲我知道的一切
沒有偉大的計畫
在日落大道上沒有新的想法
穆荷蘭大道上沒有持續太久的橋段
沒有合資企業拆夥斷裂
沒有狂野旋律在我腦海縈繞徘徊

沒有。一點消息也沒有，七點二十七分一切都不再前進
也沒那麼想吃晚餐
只聽著電視聲化成的背景音樂

我──走出車外站上露臺
思索天空暮色變化的進度
臆測道奇隊的表現何如
伸手拿了電話
打給一位老朋友。

You're only as happy as your least happy child

你的快樂只比得上你最不快樂的孩子

你以為我很富有 的確 但不是你想的那樣
我住在Mar Vista公路下的都鐸洋房
緊鄰海洋
你一打來我就將手機帶到外頭
Rose Bowl買的野餐桌
聽上方的車呼嘯而過
想起上次你來找我
我們最後一次做愛
尖峰時車聲越來越大，越來越大
大到像耳邊的一片海
這片海像極了天空
我扶搖直上 因你比我高了兩吋
直到你把我擁進懷中
我伸手就能摘下星辰
他們在我身邊一個個隕落
我成為了天使
讓你哄我上床

開心

人們以為我很富有 的確 但不是他們想的那樣
我有輛卡車 純金鑰匙圈掛在點火開關上
背面寫著：喜樂歡欣又自由
開心

我開著它時
就會想起上次陪我開車的朋友們
收音機音量開到爆表聽不見彼此說話
於是我們也成了音樂
開心

報導都說我很富有 的確 但不是他們想的那樣
我有個保險櫃我都叫它「男友箱」
裡頭收好一張張發票
一張張電影票只是提醒自己
我無條件愛過失去過又重新眷戀的那些

你開玩笑說我超有錢 的確 但不是你想的那樣
我住在高速公路底下的都鐸洋房
在羅斯大道離海不遠的地方
你打給我時我套上你的毛衣
打開擴音
在樹下和你漫聊幾晌
想到你最後一次躺在我身邊
尖峰時的車聲越來越大，越來越大
成了一條小河或激流
我倆好似在水中優遊
而這不只是一場夢
我們是真的很

開心

糖霜魚[1]

讓我來沾點甜蜜
手腳都灑上糖粉
聖文森道糖霜魚
我齒間甜甜蜜蜜
有你寄來的飛吻
電影鄰座的記憶
道奇球場思樂冰
海上的白色點心
浪花泡沫的綿密
算命師曾告訴我
讓生活充滿甜蜜　甜蜜男子會降臨。

當晚洗了蜂蜜澡
腳趾泡玫瑰紙幣
整夜身子都不起
嚥下了瓊漿玉液。

我身上滿是糖蜜
蜂兒窮追我不離
想法也更有魅力
有些陰鬱沒創意

唇啊齒啊都是蜜
指尖按著 emoji
時髦的心很堅毅
快快來呀帥baby

註：
1. 位於LA一間熱門壽司店。

我把三號手機繫在緊身褲的腰帶上
只有你知道它號碼
6 plus 震動著你專屬鈴聲
聽見你模仿小孩嬉鬧我便微笑
因我知道打來的是你
就是這些小事讓我微笑
我把它們藏在心底
我真的好喜歡你
你一沒打來我就緊張兮兮
我順著呼吸隔空對你
說別訓練我的堅毅
我真的只想脆弱溫柔
若你能讓我做我自己
你將是我生命中的唯一

在梅爾羅斯公寓

要如何我才不會覺得火車即將
離去 讓自己像個悲劇女英雄綁在末節車廂
要如何我才不會需要你
就可以輕鬆與你兒戲
放任你就是你自己

不把你當救世主
也不演歐菲莉亞的悲劇
不把我們的信仰 浪費在大眾的黑魔術裡

週日去走走好嗎？
庭院裡有兩隻貓
廣播小小聲放送
爐火在暖暖地燒
我心裡深深知道
高山深谷也阻止不了
我走過黑暗拉開與你的距離

這樣我們就不用忙著吵架討公平
不是每段婚姻都一定要崩潰叫停

我不需要你
但我想要你
因為你真的很酷
這樣我不必那麼受傷
你也不必這麼死命一意孤行
你和朋友要做什麼白日夢也是你自己的事
我倆之間這樣就很足夠
坐在梅爾羅斯的公寓裡
喀地打開大罐啤酒
一顆心正在燃燒
　我愛你喬賽亞
　很抱歉我仍帶著傷
但我還是能讓你快樂。
讓我們倒個滿杯
　敬認清彼此
　不敬痴心期望

謝謝你當地人

我一路逃離你來到箭頭湖
沒告訴你我去哪裡
知道你拍完片前 還有24小時寬限期
我去了匿名戒酒會
分享一段酷似主婦被痛毆的故事

我感覺到眾目睽睽
坐後排的復健兒童放下手上的紙團 直直盯著我看
我他媽的恨透我的人生。

活動結束後我在停車場等著 隨便一位當地女性
來和我說說話
只有Kira搭理我
她說:「我沒辦法給妳什麼建議」

我身陷絕境
無力轉圜
來到不對的地點 不對的季節 不對的時間 連表情都不對
雖然我早就知曉
但我不知道還能怎樣

你說要我嫁給你
你說你媽在垂死邊緣 你命中要有個女人才能摸透人生。

我軟了下心但這理由差強人意
我想要的不只這樣
儘管我自始至終都一無所有。
如果我想把一元鈔票換成硬幣 要徵詢意見也不知道該打給誰。

但我心中總有那麼小小的一塊
大概像天使蛋糕切下的一小塊
以某種方式感受到
我值得比你更好的一個人。

我坐上卡車周遭一片黑暗
皺巴巴的黃色小冊上有兩個號碼 我應該不會打
是Kira附上區域號碼 和她好心提供的

互助人，住棕櫚谷名叫Gale。

我的心情沒有變好也沒撥半通電話 但我覺得能在大房間裡穿著高中給的法蘭絨外套，聲淚俱下
地分享，是種盡己所能的勇敢
開口說

「 我愛的男人痛恨我
但留下來比離開容易。」

最後一臺車呼嘯而過 車燈滿溢我的擋風玻璃
夜晚從此刻起變得寧靜
我心想——

如果我回去結束關係
下次開車經過熟悉的街頭 一切都成過眼雲煙 我該如何面對
人事已非。
甜美不再。
甜美是我喚你名字嘴裡的感覺
甜美是我還年輕時，與你有說有笑開過大街小巷
那時你我之間還不用爭戰
沒人知曉你我之間
除了我們倆。

甜美一如瘋君子對愛的定義。
我以為你如我的清清白白
想靠近偉大的理想和自由。
但有些人需要有自己的祕密

而現在我最大的一場仗
就是這首奔放旋律
在我心中
開始沒有你站我隔壁。
關上門來揮別過去盲目地
前進
踏入深淵
沒有無辜的目的地
指南針上唯一的方向——前方。

於是我向前開去
來來回回
在世界公路的邊緣
她美麗的名字提醒了我

我很美麗
有些事物毫無理由地美麗。
並非每個人都需假裝愛自己的女友 就因為母親即將離去
或因為他們只是害怕季節的更替……

不論如何
我想不到完美的對句 給這首詩美麗的結局
說不出什麼大道理

除了我很有勇氣
還有留下來比離開容易

I'm writing my future

我寫著自己的未來

The universe exists
　　　　because we are aware of it

宇宙因我們
　　覺察而存在

天堂極其易碎

天堂極其易碎
一切看似只會雪上加霜
我們在佛州對抗劇毒的赤潮。
死魚遍地
更別提颶風和海平面上升不息
回到洛杉磯狀況一樣嚴峻
我的六十年樹屋吞噬在伍爾西森林大火
誰會想到你會在我三十三歲這年被奪去
在一位沉默寡言的一戰飛行員
親手搭建你之後的歲歲年年。
我試著挽救你
但馬兒和德國牧羊犬們更危急

天堂極其易碎 一切看似只會雪上加霜
我們之前就見識過 領導者是個超級自大狂
但這並非整個國家罪有應得。
朋友們叫我別再為文化拉警報
但我要不這樣要不把自己送去精神治療。
他們不懂
我是個夢想家
我對國家有許多遠大的夢想
非關她能做些什麼 而是能感受什麼
她能思索什麼 她能作什麼夢。
我知道,我知道——我何德何能為妳作夢
就只是我的心中從出生就有一小塊天堂。這點我很幸運
不像我的丈夫——出生長大都是地獄。
我總是有些溫柔能夠給予——
其實就是我全部的自己
這是我美麗的事物之一
這是人性美麗的事物之一
但最近我一直在想 但願有人在我小時告訴我 那些天堂裡予取予求的居民。他們攫取的太多
已沒什麼能夠給予。
並非所有人天性都善良無瑕

而你無法戰勝天性裡的一切。

我們在阿古拉山滅火時我一直想著這些
我已經厭倦與你爭戰。
厭倦你對我予取予求

天堂極其易碎 一切只會雪上加霜
每次你離去我似乎都會想到夏娃的咒詛
在信念滿盈的那夜
她咬下了禁果
來自結實累累的樹上
你把我吸入
昆達里尼
在這夏夜
與我相覷
然後你攫取又攫取又攫取又攫取
但你的吻活像海邊的香氣
治癒我淚眼汪汪的糖衣
在我血脈中你翻騰渲染著柑橘
毒蛇爬上橘樹的水彩畫逐漸清晰
在我心中愈發甜蜜
我開始覺得自己能永遠如此
不再猶豫
但我的心脆弱無比
已沒什麼能夠給予

沙拉曼達

滾出我的血液 沙拉曼達
我呼出的水氣沒能把你攆出腦海
踩著輪迴置你於死地
一路跑到San Pedro 把你趕出我的血液
但不管我去哪裡 你似乎形影不離。
而我也在那裡。

我不想再販賣自己的故事請別再逼我。
我想把它們收在床頭櫃自己湮沒
或在海灘狂歡後的午夜偶爾想起
或在你身邊的某個午後
快快帶過——牽著你下班後粗糙的手。

我愛你
但你並不了解我

你看我真是個詩人

我的生活是我的詩
求愛是我不朽的存在

我的想法不容販賣
它們是無目的的存在
楚楚動人不必收費

願你了解這些
能愛上我這一切

因為買不到的事物無法估量價值
而超脫人類之上。

無法企及
安全無虞
獨特且唯一

無法解碼或更替
抽象摸不著形體

就像夏日最完美的彎路上
從你車窗映入眼簾的
一幅海景

完美無瑕能幻化為
天上人間綢緞的一縷質地
就像奧林帕斯山
宙斯雅典娜和眾神的宅邸

I love u
But u don't understand me

You see
I'm a real poet

My life is my poetry
My lovemaking is my legacy

我愛你
但你並不了解我

你看
我真是個詩人

我的生活是我的詩
求愛是我不朽的存在

You can have a life beyond your wildest dreams

all you have to do is change everything...

All you have to do is change everything

All you have to do is change everything

all you have to do is change everything

你可以在最瘋狂的夢想彼端生活

只要你改變一切……

只要你改變一切

只要你改變一切

只要你改變一切

俳句

Jasmine in the air
the burden of fame is real
never felt so clear

空氣中的茉莉
聲名使我狼藉
從未如此清晰

You in the soft light
the 405 from Venice
a river of red

你在微光之中
離開威尼斯的405[1]
一條鮮紅河流

註：
1.「405」指加州405號州際公路，「威尼斯」則是加州的威尼斯海灘。

Wondering if it's
astronomical twilight
or civil twilight

疑惑這是
天文曙暮光
還是民用曙暮光

Every night I die
when I give myself to you
sad but beautiful

夜夜我都死去
向你獻出自己
悲傷卻美麗

```
Poets- like comics
are inherently quite sad
better off alone
```

詩人──就像諧星
內心充滿悲傷
隻身一人為上

I stepped on a bird
cried in my new boyfriend's arms
to live is to kill

我踩死了一隻鳥兒
在我新男友的懷裡哭泣
活著就是殺生

For years I begged you
to just take me in your arms
you wouldn't. Couldn't.

太多年來我乞求你
單單把我擁入懷
你從未如此。辦不到。

Babe let's go to town
buy something sweet - pink grapefruit
eat it with sugar

寶貝我們進城去
買些粉紅葡萄柚
拌糖吃個它甜甜蜜蜜

No big decisions
to the lake or to the sea
My only question

沒什麼大不了
去湖邊或去海邊
是我唯一的問題

Open the front door
hello I say to no one
I know no one's home

我打開了大門
對空氣打招呼
我知道，沒人在家

詩人筆記

附 錄
英 文 詩 原 稿

Violet Bent Backwards Over the Grass

I went to a party
I came in hot
made decisions beforehand
my mind made up
things that would make me happy
to do them or not
each option weighed quietly
a plan for each thought

But then i walked through the door
past the open concept

and saw Violet
        bent backwards over the grass
7 years old with dandelions grasped

                    tightly in her hands
arched like a bridge in a fallen handstand
grinning wildly like a madman
with the exuberance that only doing nothing can bring
waiting for the fireworks to begin

and in that moment
i decided to do nothing about everything

forever.

Bare feet on linoleum

Stay on your path Sylvia Plath
don't fall away like all the others

Don't take all your secrets alone to your watery grave about
lovers and mother

The secrets you keep will keep you in deep like father and Amy
and brother
And all of the people you meet on the street will reiterate lies
that she uttered

Leave me in peace I cry
late at night on a slow boat bound for Catalina for no reason

tiny beads of sweat dot my forehead
could be mistaken for dewdrops if this were photo season.

But alas this is a real life - and it's been a real fight just to
keep my mind from committing treason.
Why you ask?
Because she told the townspeople I was crazy and the lies they
started to believe them

But anyway - I've moved on now

And now that I've gone scorched-earth
I'm left wondering where to go from here.
To Sonoma where the fires have just left?
South Dakota?

Would standing in front of Mount Rushmore feel like the Great
American homecoming I never had?

Would the magnitude of the scale of the sculpture take the place
of the warm embrace I've never known?

Or should I just be here now
In the kitchen
Bare feet on linoleum
Bored - but not unhappy
Cutting vegetables over boiling water that I will later turn
into stew.

What happened when I left you

Perfect petals punctuate the fabrics yellow blue
silver platters with strawberries strewn across the room

In Zimmerman with sandals on one summer dress to choose

Three girls
eyes rolled
loud laughter
dust specks lit by afternoon

My life is sweet like lemonade now there's no bitter fruit 🌑
eternal sunshine of the spotless mind
no thought of you

My thoughts have changed
my voice is higher
now i'm over u

No flickering in my head movies
projected in Bellevue

Because I captured the mood of my wish fulfilled
and sailed to Xanadu

The grief that came in waves that rolled I navigated through

The fire from my wish as wind to a future trip to Malibu

now everything I have is perfect
nothing much to do

just perfect florals
green embroidered chairs
one dress to choose

LA Who am I to Love You?

LA, I'm from nowhere who am I to love you
LA, I've got nothing who am I to love you
when I'm feeling this way
and I've got nothing to offer
LA
not quite the city that never sleeps
not quite the city that wakes
But the city that dreams for sure
if by dreams you mean nightmares.

LA
I'm a dreamer but
I'm from nowhere who am I to dream

LA
I'm upset!
I have complaints!
Listen to me
They say I come from money and I didn't and I didn't even have
love and it's unfair

LA
I sold my life rights for a big check
but now I can't sleep at night and I don't know why
plus I love Saks so why did I do that when I know
it won't last

LA
I picked San Francisco because the man who doesn't love me
lives there

LA!
I'm pathetic
but so are you
can I come home now?

Daughter to no one
table for one
party of thousands of people I don't know at Delilah
where my ex-husband works
I'm so sick of this
But

Can I come home now?
Mother to no one
private jet for one
back home to the Tudor house that borne a thousand murder
plots
Hancock Park treated me very badly I'm resentful.

The witch on the corner
the neighbor nobody wanted
the reason for Garcetti's extra security.

LA!
I know I'm bad but I have nowhere else to go can I come
home now?
I never had a mother
will you let me make the sun my own now
and the ocean my son
I'm quite good at tending to things despite my upbringing
Can I raise your mountains?
I promise to keep them greener make them my daughters
teach them about fires warn them about water

I'm lonely LA
can I come home now?

I left my city for San Francisco
I'm writing from the golden gate bridge but it's not going
as planned
I took a free ride off a billionaire and brought my
typewriter and promised myself I would stay
but
it's just not going the way I thought
it's not that I feel different
and I don't mind that it's not hot

it's just that I belong to no one, which means
there's only one place for me
the city not quite awake
the city not quite asleep
the city that's something else- something in between
the city that's still deciding
how good it should be

and also

I can't sleep without you

No one's ever really held me like you
not quite tightly
but certainly I feel your body next to me
smoking next to me
vaping lightly next to me
and I love that you love the neon lights
like me
Orange
in the distance. We both love that and I love that we have
that in common.

Also neither one of us can go back to New York.
For you, are unmoving.
As for me, it won't be my city again until I'm dead.
Fuck the New York Post!

LAAAAA!
Who am I to need you when I've needed so much
asked for so much
what i've been given I'm not yet sure I may never know that either
until I'm dead.

For now though
what I do know is that I don't deserve you-
not you at your best, in your splendor with towering
eucalyptus trees that sway in my dominion
Not you at your worst-
totally on fire, unlivable unbreathable.
I don't deserve you at all
You see- You have a mother
A continental shelf
a larger piece of land from whence you came

And I am an orphan
a little seashell that rests upon your native shores
one of many that's for sure but because of that
I surely must love you closely to the most out of anyone.

For that reason-
Let me love you
don't mind my desperation
let me hold you not just for vacation but for real and forever
Make it real life, let me be a real wife to you.
Girlfriend, lover, mother, friend.
I adore you
Don't be put off by my quick-wordedness
I'm generally quite quiet, quite a meditator
actually I'll do very well down by Paramahansa Yogananda's
Realization center I'm sure.
I promise you'll barely even notice me

unless you want to notice me
unless you prefer a rambunctious child

in which case I can turn it on too!
I'm good on the stage as you may know, you may have heard of me?

So either way I'll fit in just fine
so just love me by doing nothing
except for perhaps by not shaking the county line.
I'm yours if you'll have me
quietly or loudly
sincerely your daughter
regardless
you're mine.

The Land of 1000 fires

Two blue steel trains run through the tunnels of your
cool blue steel eyes
Vernon
Rock quarry
The vastness of which has nothing on my beautiful mind
Dylan
i hear Dylan when i look at you
i can see it on my arm in invisible ink like a tattoo
The yin to my yang
the toughness to my unending softness
A striking example of masculinity
firm in your verticality
sure in your confrontation against all elements
and duality
The sun to my wilting daisy
The earth to the wildflower that doesn't care where it grows

Vernon
everything's burnt here
there's no escaping it
the air is fried and on fire
I've never really fallen in love
but whatever this feeling is
i wish everyone could experience it
this place feels like a person
familiar
like someone i've stood next to before
but never while i was standing next to you
Thank you
for being here
for bearing witness to my vastness

Through the years I've called you in and out of my orbit
You, in your madness
the satellite that's constellating my World
mimicking the inner chaos that i've disowned
a mirror to my past life retribution
a reflection of my sadness
If i'm going to keep on living the way that i'm living
i can't do it without you.
My feet aren't on the ground
i need your body to stand on
your name to define me
on top of being a woman
i am scared
and
ethereal
and

there are seven worlds in my eyes

i'm accessing all of them at once

one to draw my words from and my muses
another one i try and harness late at night that lies somewhere
off of the right of Jupiter
and then of course there's this one i live in
the land of 1,000 fires
that's where you come in

You
Vernon
Dylan
Two blue steel trains
running through the tunnels of your
cool blue steel eyes

to guide me far from the world of my early days
that i can't quite make out clearly
that beckon me toward high sea cliffs
on long car rides

toward a future place
a world unknown to me
made up of something surreal and dripping
Flowers in solar systems Oversized

You Vernon Dylan

no words needed to sponge up the
dark nights
no explanation for the globes in my eyes
shoulder to shoulder in the factory light
letting me be who i would have been
if everything had turned out alright

3 alternative endings
course through my blood on ice

i thrive because i say i do
and because it's what i write

But honestly if you weren't here
i don't know what things would look like

That's why no matter what world i'm in
i navigate by satellite
Vernon
Dylan
and you in your madness

two trains running
through your cool blue eyes

Never to Heaven

May my eyes always stay level to the horizon
may they never gaze as high as heaven
to ask why
The whys in this lifetime i've found
are inconsequential compared to the magic of the nowness
~~which is~~ the solution to most questions   *So as to have to ask*
    May i never go where angels fear to tread - To make the fool fgs zesun
there are no reasons   *in the sky*
and if there are, i'm wrong.
But at least i won't have spent my life waiting
looking for god in the clouds of the dawn
listening out for otherworldly contact
30 billion light years on

No I'll let the others do the pondering
and while they do i'll be on my lawn
reading something unsubstantial with the television on

i'll be up early to rise though of course-
but only to make you a pot of coffee

That's what i was thinking this morning Joe-
that it's times like this
as the marine layer lifts
off the sea from the view of our favorite restaurant
that i pray that i may always keep my eyes level to your
eye line
never downcast at the table cloth
too nervous to share my innermost thoughts
with you

You see Joe
it's times like this as the marine layer lifts
off the sea on the dock where we're standing *w/the candle lit*
that i think to myself
there's things you still don't know about me
like sometimes i'm afraid my sadness is too big
and that one day you might have to help me handle it
but until then-

May i always keep my eyes level to this skyline
assessing the glittering new development
off the coast of Long Beach
never to heaven

Because i have faith in man as strange as that seems
in times like these
and it's not just because of the warmth i've found in your
brown eyes-
it's because I believe in the goodness in me
that it's firm enough to plant a flag in
or a rosebud
or to build a new life.

Never to Heaven

May my eyes always stay level to the horizon
may they never gaze as high as heaven
to ask why
May I never go where angels fear to tread
so as to have to ask for answers in the sky
The whys in this lifetime i've found are inconsequential
compared to the magic of the nowness- the solution to most
questions
there are no reasons.
and if there are- i'm wrong
but at least i won't have spent my life waiting
looking for God in the clouds of the dawn
or listening out for otherworldly contact
30 billion light years on
No. i'll let the others do the pondering
while i'll be sitting on the lawn
reading something unsubstantial
with the television on
I'll be up early to rise though of course-
but only to make you a pot of coffee
That's what i was thinking this morning Joe
that it's times like this as the marine layer lifts
off the sea from the view of our favorite restaurant
that i pray that i may
always keep my eyes level to your eyeline
never downcast at the tablecloth
Yes Joe
it's times like this as the marine layer lifts
off the sea on the dock with the candle lit
that i think to myself
there are things you still don't know about me
like sometimes i'm afraid my sadness is too big
and that one day you might have to help me handle it

but until then
may i always keep my eyes level to this skyline
assessing the glittering new development
off of the coast of Long Beach
never to heaven or revenant
Because i have faith in man as strange as that seems
in times like these
and it's not just because of the warmth i've found in your
brown eyes
but because i believe in the goodness in me
that it's firm enough to plant a flag in
or a
rosebud
or to build a new life.

Tessa DiPietro

No one ever touched me without wanting to kill me
except for a healer on 6th Street and Ridgeley

Tessa DiPietro recommended casually
by a medium i no longer know

She said my number one problem was my field was untrusting
when asked what to do she paused and said
nothing
which sent me right into uncontrollable sobbing
because there's never anything you can do about the important
things

She said
Ok, one thing you can do is
picture the floor rising up to support you
and sink into the back of the bed that's behind you
too much of your energy is in front of and above you

Which for some reason made me think of a live show i had seen
Jim Morrison at the Hollywood Bowl
1968? (check date)
the blue trellised lights gave him an unusual aura
like a halo or something- made him 8 feet or taller
i remember just thinking he looked out of his body
but definitely like a God on stage

So i told her
Maybe an artist has to function a little bit above themselves
if they really want to transmit some heaven

Then she told me
Singleness of focus is the key to transmission
for an emphasis on developing inner intuition
close your eyes and feel where you hold your attention
if it's in the back of your eyes walk it down to your heart
center
and make that the new place from which your thoughts enter
clairvoyance comes mostly from this simple function

Oh- and Jim died at 27
so find another frame of reference when you're referencing
heaven
And did you ever read the lyrics to 'People Are Strange'?
He made no sense.

                    Past the bushes Cypress thriving

I saw you in the mirror
you were wearing your hair differently
carrying the air differently
You say you want your hair long parted in the middle
Long in solidarity - worn for all his women

Long Beach

Aimless

your fingers wiping oil on the paper w precision
w decision like an artist never seen yet with a vision

W a reason
Stared w venom at the ceiling
not the grass
but straight ahead
Just at the skyline
w precision
laser vision

time was stopping
moving through u.
U dictated
by what moved u

   only moving never thinking

Match the sun that's slowly sinking
at the height of afternoon
In the heat of summer evening
Like a phoenix like a chemtrail like a wavelength No
one's claiming

Georgia O'Keeffe
Georgia peaches
Doing nothing but your painting
For forever
Forget teachers
Forgive him for ever leaving

love is rising
No resisting
cheeks are flushing
Now you're living

Say goodbye now
 no resisting
Live your life like
 no one's listening

Be the art that life is breathing
Be the soul the world is living.

Do what you want
For you only
Not for giving
Just for taking
No one's listening

at the end of Lime and 10th street down the road that's green
and winding
        Past the bushes cypress thriving past the chain
link fence
  and driving
            farther down the road less traveled
         there u are athleisure wear unraveled
Now I see you clear

Standing stoic blue and denim
eyes not blue but clear like
heaven

you don't want to be forgotten

You just want to disappear

SportCruiser

I took a flying lesson on my 33rd birthday instead of calling you
or parking on the block where our old place used to be
Genesee
Genesee
Genesee
Pathetic I know, but sometimes I still like to park on that street
and have lunch in the car just to feel close to you.
I was once in love with my life here
in that studio apartment with you
little yellow flowers on the tops of trees as our only view
out of the only window- big enough for me to see our future
through.
But it turned out I was the only one who could see it.
Stupid apartment complex. Terrible you. You who i wait for
               You

               You

               You
Like a broken record stuck on loop.

So that day on my birthday i thought something has to change,
it can't always be about waiting for u

Don't tell anyone but
part of my reasoning for taking the flight class was this idea
that if i could become my own navigator- a captain of the sky
that perhaps i could stop looking for direction- from you.

Well, what started off as an idea on a whim has turned into
something more. Too shy to explain to the owners that my first
lesson was just a one time thing. I've continued to go to classes
each week. At the precious little strip off of Santa Monica
and Bundy.
And everything was going fine we were starting with dips and
loops. And then something terrible happened-
during my fourth lesson in the sky, my instructor-
younger than i but as tough as you- instructed me to do a
simple maneuver. It's not that i didn't do it but i was
slow to lean the SportCruiser into a right hand upward turn.
Scared. Scared that i would lose control of the plane
Not tactfully and not gently the instructor shook his head
and without looking at me said, "you don't trust yourself."
I was horrified. Feeling as though I had somehow been found out.

Like he knew me- how weak i was

 Of course he was only talking about my ability as a pilot
in the sky. But i knew it was meant for me to hear those words.
for me they held a deeper meaning.
I didn't trust myself
not just 2500 ft above the coast of Malibu
but with anything. And i didnt trust you,
I could have said something but i was quiet
because pilots aren't like poets
they don't make metaphors between life and the sky.

In the midst of this midlife meltdown navigational exercise
in self-examination, I also decided to do something else I
always wanted to do- take sailing lessons in the vibrant bay
of Marina Del Rey. I signed up for the class as Elizabeth
Grant and nobody blinked an eye. So why was I so sure that
when I walked into the tiny shack on Bali Way someone would
say "you're not a captain of a ship or the master of the sky"
No, the fisherman didn't care and so neither did I.
And for a brief moment i felt more myself than ever before,
letting the self-proclaimed drunkard captain's lessons wash
over me like the foamy tops of the sea.
Midway through, my forehead burned and my hands raw from
jibing, the captain told me the most important thing i would
need to know on the sea. Never run the ship into irons.
That's nautical terms for not sailing the boat directly into
the wind. In order to do that though you have to know where
the wind is coming from. And you might not have time to look
to the mast or up farther to the weather vane
so you have to feel where the wind is coming from-
on your cheeks, and by the tips of the white waves-
from which direction they're rolling.
To do this, he gave me an exercise.
He told me to close my eyes and asked me to feel on my neck
which way the wind was blowing. I already knew I was going
to get it wrong.
"The wind is coming from everywhere- I feel it all over."
I told him.
"No," he said. "The wind is coming from the left. The port side."
I sat waiting for him to tell me,"you don't trust yourself."
But he didn't, so I said it for him.
"I don't trust myself."
He laughed, gentler than the pilot but still not realizing
that my failure in the exercise was hitting me at a much
deeper level.
"It's not that you don't trust yourself," he said. "It's simply
that you're not a captain. It isn't what you do."
Then he told me he wanted me to practice every day so I would
get better.
"Which grocery store do you go to?" he asked
"To the Ralphs in the Palisades," I replied.
"Ok. When you're in the Ralphs in the Palisades - I want you-
as you're walking from your car to the store - to close your
eyes and feel which way the wind is blowing. Now I don't
want you to look like a crazy person crouching in the middle
of the parking lot but everywhere you go- I want you to
try and find which way the wind is coming in from and then determine
if it's from the port or starboard side so when you're
back on the boat you'll have a better sense of it."
I thought his advice was adorable. I could already picture
myself in the parking lot squinting my eyes with perfect
housewives looking on. I could picture myself growing a
better sense of which way the wind was blowing and as I did
a tiny bit of deeper trust also began to grow within myself.

I thought of mentioning it but I didn't.
Because captains aren't like poets
they don't make metaphors between the sea and sky.
And as I thought that to myself
I realized-
that's why I write.

All of this circumnavigating the earth
was to get back to my life
6 trips to the moon for my poetry to arise
I'm not a captain
I'm not a pilot
I write
I write.

Quiet Waiter- Blue forever

   You move like water sweet baby sweet waiter
making the night smile to no one you xcater
   quiet wood worker from midnight till later
   my lover my laughter my armor my maker
   The way that I feel with you is something like aching
   inside my stomach the cosmos are baking
   A universe hung like a mobile
   the alignment of these planets unique
   In me the earth moves around the sun
   no land all sea

   water world
   sun chaser
   tropic of cancer
   southern equater
   i'm the crying crustacean
   sunbathing on paper
   moon.
   Let's rewrite the beginning of this primordial ooze
   shall we my love?
   Am i being brazen for saying this year makes me feel
   like we could've wrote it better
   than him (rhyme w Moon?)
   But who am I   dreaming on paper
   just a girl in love scribbling in journals
   rearranging the salt and pepper
                                me
   in love with you
   my ~~blue~~ quiet waiter
   ~~forever~~
   summer
   ~~quiet waiter~~
   weather Blue forever ?
   Call me when you're done with work/ the darker the better
   i'll pick you up later

Quiet Waiter Blue Forever

You move like water sweet baby sweet waiter
making the night smile to no one you cater
silent woodworker from midnight till later
my lover my laughter my armor my maker
The way that i feel with you is something like aching
inside of my stomach the cosmos are baking
a universe hung like a mobile
the alignment of these planets unique
in me the earth moves around the sun
no land all sea
water world
sun chaser
tropic of cancer
southern equator
i'm the crying crustacean
sunbathing on paper
moon.
Let's rewrite the beginning of this primordial ooze
shall we my love
Am i being brazen for saying this year makes me feel
like we could've written it better
than him?
But who am i
just a girl in love dreaming on paper
rearranging the salt for the pepper
in love with you
my quiet waiter
Summer
blue
Forever
call me when you're done with work
i'll pick you up later
the darker the better
five after midnight
the darker the better

My bedroom is a sacred place now - There are children
            at the foot of my bed

Last year when I wrote you my last letter
(the beginning of my future poetry)
I acknowledged who you were for the first time.
I didn't call you by any other name
I let you know that I knew the true nature of your heart-
that it was evil
that it convinced me that darkness is real
that the devil is a real devil
and that monsters don't always know they are monsters.

But projection is an interesting thing
after you burned the house down
you tried to convince me that i was the one holding the
matches
You told me that I din't know what I had done
You said I don't know who I am

But I do know who I am.

I love Rose Gardens
I buy violets every time someone leaves me
I love the great sequoias of Yosemite
and if you asked my sister to describe the first thing she
thinks of when she thinks of me
she would say
woodsmoke

I'm gentle
I'm funny
when I'm drunk
though I haven't been drunk for 14 years

I go on trips to the beach with my friends who don't know
that I'm crazy.
I can do that.
I can do anything-
even leave you

because my bedroom is a sacred place now
there are children at the foot of my bed
telling me stories about the friends they pretend to hate
that they will make up with tomorrow-
and there are fresh cut flowers that i grew myself
in vases on nightstands hand-carved by old pals from Big Sur
and the longer i stay here, the more i am sure
that the more i step into becoming a poet the less
i will fall into being with you
the more i step into my poetry the less i will fall into
being with you
            the more i step into
                    my poetry the less i will
fall into being with you
        the more i step into my poetry the less i will
  fall into being
                with you

the
   more
        i step into becoming a poet
the less i will fall into
bed
with
   you.

In the hills of Benedict Canyon

Love has room to grow in the hills of Benedict Canyon
My green typewriter light is on
and two months' time between me and my last man
No double murder plots looming over neighbors' vacant lots
that i look upon at twilight, still light enough for the
Starline bus to be carrying on. I listen to the hippie
spouting nonsense at the foot of Bella Drive
hammering on about Sharon and the sanctity of life
I listen on intently
thanks for the free ride
and for reminding me that everything comes down to a story
and to laugh when you could cry.

But finally I have no reason for tears
not tonight at 7:27
first time in months i feel close to heaven
in the hills of Benedict Canyon
the background hum of the television
love has room to grow.
No more secrets no more reasons to put off what I already know
No more big projects
no new dev breaking ground on Sunset
no big builds lasting too long up on Mulholland
no joint ventures fracturing.
no unchained melodies enchanting the bars in my head.

No. Just no news, nothing going on at 7:27
not quite ready for dinner
the background hum of television

Me- standing out on the deck
wondering what phase of twilight the sky is in
and contemplating how the Dodgers are doing
and reaching for the phone
to call an old friend.

happy

you thought i was rich and i am but not how you think
i live in a Tudor house under the freeway in Mar Vista
by the beach
when you call i take my phone outside to the picnic table
that i bought from the Rose Bowl
and i listen to the rushing cars above
and think about the last time you visited me
the last time we made love
how the noise got louder and louder during rush hour
until it sounded like the sea
and it felt like the ocean was the sky
and that i was flying because you were two feet taller than me
until you took me in your arms
and i could touch the stars
and they all fell down around my head
and i became an angel
and you put me to bed

happy

People think that i'm rich and i am but not how they think
i have a truck with a gold key chain in the ignition
and on the back it says: happy joyous and free

happy

and when i drive
i think about the last time my friends were driving with me
how the radio was so loud that we couldn't hear the words
so we became the music

happy

They write that i'm rich and i am but not how they think
i have a safe i call the boyfriend box
and in it every saved receipt
every movie theater ticket just to remind me
of all the things i've loved and lost and loved again
unconditionally

You joke that i'm rich and i am but not how you think
i live in a Tudor house under the freeway
off of Rose Avenue 12 blocks from the beach
and when you call i put your sweater on
and put you on speaker
and chat for hours underneath the trees
and think about the last time you were here lying next to me
how the noise from the cars got louder and louder
during rush hour
until it sounded like a river or a stream
and it felt like we were swimming
but it wasn't just a dream
we were just

happy

Sugarfish

Lemme stick to something sweet
sugar on my hands and feet
Sugarfish San Vicente
sugar sugar in my teeth
from your kiss you texting me
from the movie theater seat
Dodger Stadium Slurpee
white confection in the sea
powder waves froth over me
A fortune teller once told me
do things that you think are sweet and a sweet man is sure to
follow.

So I made a bath that night of honey
dipped my toes in rose and money
stayed all night in that bathwater
even some I swallowed.

Now there's so much sugar on me
I can't keep the bees off of me
even most of my thoughts are charming
some are blue and borrowed

Sugar sugar lips and teeth
fingertips touch emojis
hard forever
hearts on fleek
bb please come over

ringtone

I put my third phone in the waistband of my leggings
only u have this number
6 plus vibrates with your own ringtone
i smile when i hear simulated children laughing
cause i know it's u
it's the little things that make me smile
i keep them just for myself
i like u so much
but it makes me nervous when u don't call
under my breath i say
Don't make me be resilient
i so want to be soft
if u let me be myself
u will be the first one who ever did.

In the flats of Melrose

What will it take for me not to feel like the train will
run away with me bound up like the sad heroine tied to the last
car
What will it take for me not to need you
so I can just have you for fun
and for who you really are

Not you as the savior
not me as Ophelia
not us putting our faith in the public's dark art

Topanga on Sunday?
two cats in the yard
NPR rumbling quietly
a fire in the hearth
me with a knowingness deep in my heart
that nothing could stop me no valley too far
to walk through in darkness to keep us apart.

And that we don't need fighting to find resolution
that not every marriage ends in the dissolution

that I don't need you
but I want you
because you're so cool
and I'm not that damaged
and ur not hell-bent on being some indie director
or whatever pipe dream you and your friends are smoking
That it's enough just for us
to be sitting in the flats of Melrose
my heart on fire
a tallboy cracked open
 I love you Josiah
 I'm sorry I'm still broken
but I could still make you happy.
Let's pour one out
 to knowing
 not hoping

Thanks to the Locals

I ran away from you to Lake Arrowhead
I didn't tell you where I was going
I knew I had a 24 hour grace period before you were done making
your film
I went to an aa meeting
And my share read like a tale of a battered housewife

I felt everyone's eyes on me
The rehab kids in the back row stopped throwing spitballs at
each other and stared at me
I fucking hate my life.

I waited after the meeting in the parking lot for any of the
local ladies
to come up to me
Only one did, Kira.
"I don't really have much advice for you" she said

I was in over my head
out of my league
In the wrong place wrong season wrong time wrong face
and I knew it
But I didn't know what to do

You asked me to marry you
You said your mother was dying and you couldn't fathom your
life without a woman in it.

I was tempted but it didn't seem like a good enough offer
I wanted more than that
even though I've never had anything.
Not one person to call if I changed my dollar in for quarters to
ask what they thought about it.

But there's always been just a little tiny piece of me inside
the size of a small slice of angel cake that knew
somewhere somehow
That I deserved better than someone like you.

So I got back into my truck in the dark
my little yellow pamphlet with two numbers on it that I would
never call crumpled up
Kira with her local area code and gratefully also her

sponsor, Gail from Palmdale.

I didn't feel better and I didn't use the numbers but I thought
that I had been very brave that I did the best I could, sharing
in a big room, tears streaming down my face in my high school
flannel
just to say

"The man that I love hates me.
But it would be easier to stay."

As the last person's lights flooded over my windshield
the night became very quiet
and i thought-

If I go back and I end it
How would I handle driving down your street and it becoming a
distant memory
not reality
no longer sweet.
Sweet the way it tastes in my mouth to say your name
sweet like when I was young, driving down those roads before we
were done
before any big battles were lost or won
unbeknownst to everyone
except for you and me.

As Sweet as a junkie's limited concept of love can be.
I thought cause u were clean u were a lot like me
wanting to be closer to something big and free.
But some people need their secrets

And now my greatest battle will be
this unchained melody
In my heart
From not having you next to me.
To shut the door on the past and step
blindly
into the abyss
no destination intact
the only direction set in the Compass - to move forward.

So I drove
back and forth
on the Rim of the World Hwy
and the beauty of its name reminded me

That I was beautiful
That some things are beautiful for no reason.
Not everyone needs to pretend to love their girlfriend just
because their mother is dying
or because they're afraid of a change in season...

Anyway
I don't have a pretty couplet to give resolution to this poem
nothing very eloquent to say

except that I was brave
and it would've been easier to stay

Paradise is Very Fragile

Paradise is very fragile
and it seems like it's only getting worse
down here in Florida we are fighting toxic red tides.
Massive fish kills
Not to mention hurricanes and rising sea levels
Back in Los Angeles things aren't looking much better
my tree house that had been standing for 60 years succumbed to
the Woolsey fires
who would've thought this year at 33 you would be taken out
from under me
after all those years
built from the ground up by hand by your very first owner.
Quiet World War 1 aviation pilot
I tried to save you
but the horses and german shepherds were more important

Paradise is very fragile and it seems that it's only
getting worse
Our leader is a megalomaniac and we've seen that before
but never because it was what the country deserved.
My friends tell me to stop calling 911 on the culture
but it's either that or I 5150 myself.
They don't understand
I'm a dreamer
And I had big dreams for the country
Not for what it could do but for how it could feel
How it could think how it could dream.
I know I know -who am I to dream for you
it's just that in my own mind I was born with a little bit of
paradise. I was lucky in that way
not like my husband- who was born and raised in hell.
I always had something gentle to give-
all of me in fact
it's one of the beautiful things about me
it's one of the beautiful things about nature
But lately I've been thinking that I wish someone had told me
when I was younger more about the inhabitants that thrive off
of paradise. That should they take too much there will be
nothing left to give.
Not everyone's nature is good or golden

and you can't fight what's in your nature.

That's all I kept thinking as we were fighting the fires
in Agoura
That I'm tired of fighting you.
Tired of you taking from me

Paradise is very fragile and it's only getting worse
and every time you leave I seem to think about the curse
bestowed upon Eve
that faithful eve
she took that bite
from that fruitful tree
You breathe me in
kundalini
on this summer night
you in front of me
And you take and you take and you take and you take
but you taste like the beach in a kiss
candy for my watery eyes
in my veins that roll you run citrus
watercolor images of serpents on orange trees quietly arise
and grow sweet in my midst
And I keep thinking I could do this forever
just like this
but my heart is very fragile
and I have nothing left to give

Salamander

Get out of my blood salamander
I can't seem to blow off enough steam to get you out of my head
SoulCycle you to death
run you out of my blood to San Pedro
and yet everywhere I go it seems there you are.
And there I am.

I don't want to sell my stories anymore stop pushing me.
I want to leave them underneath the nightstand to be forgotten
or remembered should my thoughts come upon them in the middle
of the night after a beach day
or by you some afternoon-
to thumb through- with your worn warm after-work hands.

I love u
But you don't understand me

You see I'm a real poet

My life is my poetry
my lovemaking is my legacy

My thoughts are not for sale
they're about nothing
and beautiful and for free

i wish you could get that
and love that about me

because things that can't be bought can't be evaluated
and that makes them beyond human reach.

Untouchable
Safe
Otherworldly

Unable to be deciphered or metabolized
something metaphysical

Like a view of the sea
on a summer day on the most perfect winding road
taken in from your car seat window

A thing perfect and ready to become a part of the texture of
the fabric of Something more ethereal
like Mount Olympus
where Zeus and Athena and the rest of the immortals play

館系：嬉文化

薇奧菈在草地嬉戲：拉娜‧德芮詩集【獨家中英對照版】
Violet Bent Backwards Over The Grass

作者／拉娜‧德芮 Lana Del Rey
譯者／冷月

榮譽發行人／黃鎮隆
總　經　理／陳君平
協　　　理／洪琇菁
總　編　輯／呂尚燁
主　　　編／劉銘廷
美 術 總 監／沙雲佩
美 術 主 編／李政儀
公 關 宣 傳／楊玉如、洪國瑋
國 際 版 權／黃令歡、梁名儀
文 字 校 對／施亞蒨
內 文 排 版／尚騰印刷事業有限公司

出版
城邦文化事業股份有限公司　尖端出版
台北市104中山區民生東路二段141號10樓
電話：（02）2500-7600　傳真：（02）2500-2683
讀者服務信箱：spp_books@mail2.spp.com.tw

發行
英屬蓋曼群島商家庭傳媒股份有限公司
城邦分公司　尖端出版行銷業務部
台北市104中山區民生東路二段141號10樓
電話：（02）2500-7600　傳真：（02）2500-1979
劃撥專線：（03）312-4212
劃撥帳號：50003021
戶名：英屬蓋曼群島商家庭傳媒〔股〕公司城邦分公司
※劃撥金額未滿500元，請加付掛號郵資50元
法律顧問
王子文律師　元禾法律事務所　台北市羅斯福路三段三十七號十五樓

臺灣地區總經銷
◎中彰投以北（含宜花東）　楨彥有限公司
電話：（02）8919-3369　傳真：（02）8914-5524
地址：新北市新店區寶興路45巷6弄7號5樓
物流中心：新北市新店區寶興路45巷6弄12號1樓
◎雲嘉以南　威信圖書有限公司
（ 嘉義公司 ）電話：0800-028-028　傳真：（05）233-3863
（ 高雄公司 ）電話：0800-028-028　傳真：（07）373-0087

馬新地區經銷
城邦（ 馬新 ）出版集團　Cite（ M ）Sdn.Bhd.
電話：（ 603 ）9057-8822　傳真：（ 603 ）9057-6622
E-mail：cite@cite.com.my

香港地區總經銷
城邦（ 香港 ）出版集團　Cite（ H.K. ）Publishing Group Limited
電話：852-2508-6231　傳真：852-2578-9337
E-mail：hkcite@biznetvigator.com

ISBN 978-626-308-974-7
2022年3月1版1刷　Printed in Taiwan

國家圖書館出版品預行編目(CIP)資料

薇奧菈在草地嬉戲：拉娜‧德芮詩集【獨家中英對
照版】／拉娜‧德芮(Lana Del Rey)作；冷月譯. -- 1
版. -- 臺北市：城邦文化事業股份有限公司尖端出版
：英屬蓋曼群島商家庭傳媒股份有限公司城邦分公司
發行, 2022.03
　　面；　公分
　　譯自：Violet bent backwards over the grass
　　ISBN 978-626-308-974-7(精裝)

874.51　　　　　　　　　　　　　　　　110010509

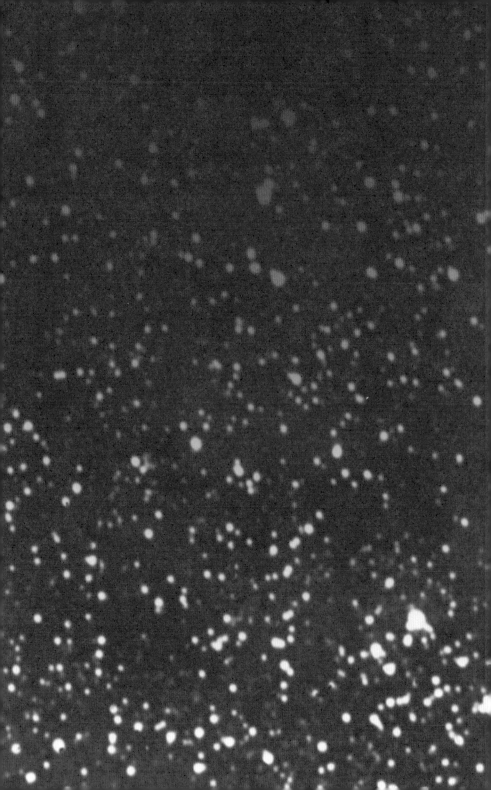

在沒有明天的狂亂中漫舞

HUSH、鄭宜農、徐珮芬、盛浩偉、潘柏霖

五位台灣創作者與詩人，書寫五篇關於他們的拉娜‧德芮

目錄

HUSH
快樂女孩在悲傷的派對　　0 0 9

鄭宜農
這樣的開心，我懂　　0 1 3

徐珮芬
我們沒有理由拒絕拉娜・德芮：讀《薇奧菈在草地嬉戲》　　0 2 3

盛浩偉
風格即詩意：讀拉娜・德芮《薇奧菈在草地嬉戲》　　0 3 1

潘柏霖
著火的屋子與忘記逃跑的人　　0 3 7

快樂女孩在悲傷的派對

語言是一件很有趣的事。

有時候同樣的意思，透過不同的語系表達，就會長成「仔細一點看還是能發現不同」的兩個相似的人。

從手中的翻譯詩，一路乘著她的音樂，飛過語系、飛過太平洋板塊，遇上Lana Del Rey，遇上一個快樂女孩在悲傷的派對。派對上悲傷的一切以震耳的分貝紮實地圍堵所有情緒的出口。城市的集合噪音、高速公路的吵雜、伴著閃光的快門聲……你能感覺得到她在試著翻譯這一切，試圖抓出其中任何帶有快樂意味的字根字首。儘管字尾可能仍然哀愁，她仍嘗試在音樂之外，以詩集的語言化整、表達那些需要理解／被理解的情緒。

於是快樂和悲傷開始長得有點相似，像一面鏡子反映出平行又翻轉的世界，而那也許同時是許多明星在成名後多半得要面對的一種虛實。

然而鏡子前的我們又何嘗不是身處在這樣的虛實之中？生活裡一面又一面鏡子，一如她的夏日哀愁（Summertime Sadness），種種電氣幻夢鏡射，像詩詞被印在紙張上，以各種不同的角度，吸收著午後悶熱的濕氣，又隨閱讀蒸發散溢在空間裡，如此往復，將我們包裹在她的音樂，她的詩集，她的悲傷派對之中。

這樣的開心，我懂

鄭宜農

二○一二年春，《Born To Die》舉著「英國金榜」的旗幟挺進世界各大通路，不久後，Lana Del Rey這個名字也開始在台灣藝文圈裡口耳相傳。原是來自美國紐約州的天主教家庭，父親從事科技業，在使用了數個藝名發表作品後，最終卻是以六○年代女伶之姿，從英國紅回好萊塢。封面上大大的半身照頂著一臉濃豔與驕傲，戲劇性的嗓音從最無所謂的呢喃到最嬌豔的吶喊之間，像是瞬間自底線刺穿頂部的曲線圖，銳角的角度大概是十五度那麼窄。

不知道有多少年輕女孩像我一樣，總之我是真心受到了影響。世界彼端，這位不過比我大兩歲的女性，在歌詞中描繪紙醉金迷的世界裡，取悅與被取悅，以及活著與死亡之間的虛線，那樣的人生際遇與相對應的膽量，是如此遙遠而陌生。我最欽羨的，是她可以擁有歌頌愛情瘋狂面的自信，畢竟當時的我，還是個寫了一張專輯裡面沒有半首情歌的懵懂少女。

因爲要寫這篇序文，多年以後的某個夏日午間，聽著至今仍然最喜歡的〈Summertime Sadness〉，我讀起這位女歌手的詩。

以〈薇奧菈在草地嬉戲〉作爲開場，場景一：派對，「好萊塢悲歌女王」風格立現。詩詞節奏可比綿密歌詞，單字是口語的，完全能想像怎麼入歌。我發現自己很快被吸引，在腦袋裡建構著與文字美感有關的讚詞，卻隨即意識到，與歌不同之處在於，觸動我的並非她筆下的那些當下。它們其實如此平淡，可是，下一秒起我們看不見的、充滿想像力的未來，正在詩句裡發生。這是我第一次意識到，Lana Del Rey的魅力並不侷限於熱烈的姿態，她的詩裡有空間，讓讀者止不住猜測薇奧菈與筆者各自的明天。

當然，如果要說整本書的刺點，大家勢必得討論起〈LA，我哪有資格愛你〉。她寫作夢之人隻身娛樂大城裡的迷茫，如同身爲女性歌者長期以來備受爭

014

議的歌詞，視角總帶著那麼一點卑微，甘願爲愛臣服。與歌不同之處在於，這詩篇裡語氣在無助中更多了諷刺，以哀求爲基底其實是則則控訴。畢竟，比起男人，LA更像是她所愛一切的載體，它太過巨大並且殘酷，很難想像做了多少犧牲才能愛得起。

而這位創作者的起點，卻是那樣擺明地爲愛而活。

查詢這將近十年光陰，Lana Del Rey與娛樂產業之間的關係，雖然看到在Twitter上公開使用巫術詛咒川普的新聞時，我是真的有笑出來，不過風雨看似精彩，實則卻也不太令人意外，大概就跟其他你想得到名字的榜上巨星一般，大家各有各的爭議，各有各的戲劇性以及相對應的黑暗。

每次看到這類新聞，我總是止不住去想：這些人也不過是眞心渴望著被愛。

在這裡，就要來談談本書到目前爲止，我最喜歡的一首詩——〈開心〉了。

你一打來我就將手機帶到外頭

我住在Mar Vista公路下的都鐸洋房 緊鄰海洋

你以為我很富有 的確 但不是你想的那樣

多麼深刻的開頭，幾句話便道盡身於他人的想像與眞實自我之間，那份渴望

平凡的脆弱，以及接近平凡的欣喜。文字堆疊著場景由遠到近，緊接著一個動作

就讓故事完整了，簡直堪稱一場寫得太好的戲。是啊，物質層面的富有都不能填滿之處，只要一通所愛之人的電話，千頭萬緒便瞬間湧出。

其後她再用下一場戲描寫生活，她寫道：

人們以為我很富有　的確　但不是他們想的那樣

我有輛卡車　純金鑰匙圈掛在點火開關上

背面寫著：喜樂歡欣又自由

開心

我開著它時　就會想起上次陪我開車的朋友們

收音機音量開到爆表聽不見彼此說話

於是我們也成了音樂

開心

確實，最開心莫過於此。一小段時間能夠心無懸念，不必擔心自己是誰、應該扮演誰，而能在自己喜歡的地方，例如一台行走中的車上，和三兩好友一起猖狂。

而最後，一路追求著愛情的女孩，經歷幾段外人臆測起來總是充滿戲劇性的獲得與失去，最終在三十六歲的年頭，寫下這樣的字句：

想到你最後一次躺在我身邊

尖峰時的車聲越來越大，越來越大

成了一條小河或激流

我倆好似在水中優遊

而這不只是一場夢

我們是真的很

開心

從享受著對外人而言幾乎可以說是屈就的愛情，在描述了千百種權勢景象，

並把墮落與暴力美學提升爲讚揚等，種種濃郁、刺激的創作之後，Lana Del

Rey用她的詩詞，或許不經意地宣示著自己新階段的開展。

而多年以前，曾經對遠方極端的形象心生嚮往的我，雖然可能永遠無法想像在比台灣大一百倍的全球娛樂產業裡浮沈的滋味，不過身為一個終於曉得什麼是愛，並且也用自己的方式，轟轟烈烈愛過的女性創作者，總覺得自己應該可以說：這樣的詩，我懂。

我們沒有理由拒絕拉娜・德芮：
讀《薇奧菈在草地嬉戲》

徐珮芬

一名女子從遠方朝向你走來，面貌模糊。她身上穿著一件花色活潑的洋裝，色彩鮮明，第一眼就給你強烈的印象。

後來，你試圖重述那個魔幻時刻，就像是垂死之人曾為隻字片語甦醒。那女人經過你身邊的時候並不看向你，但她在你耳邊低聲呢喃了幾句——那包含了你常聽說、卻不真的那麼熟悉的地名，例如仙納度，例如紐約；你的雙腳未曾親自踏上那些土地，你也不曾體驗在金門大橋上寫作的生活——然而，拉娜·德芮都告訴你了，以她萊姆氣泡水般的迷幻嗓音。

為了好好傾聽這樣的聲音，你必須找回自己的耳朵。在《薇奧菈在草地嬉戲》中，讀者可以近距離觀察拉娜·德芮面對花花世界的姿態：以一種絕對真誠的無所事事，抵禦大大小小的莫可奈何。她並不以為恥——她富有，但不如外人

想像中的富有；她執迷不悟，但還沒放棄虛度時光的能力。在擁有一切之後，她依然是那個可以在海堤坐下來，安靜一整個下午的詩人。

《薇奧菈在草地嬉戲》是拉娜‧德芮的第一本詩集。在這本書之前，她毫無疑問已是一個完熟的歌手了，沒人有資格質疑她的藝術家身分。這本原創詩集中，收錄了十四首完整作品，以及一些短篇。身為讀者，我們是否可能暫時忘卻她魔性的聲音，和那些喧嘩擾攘的爭議，將這本詩集視為一個徹底獨立的文學生命？我懷抱著這樣的好奇，我想知道答案。

濃烈如海上落日的情感，在女巫的囈語中緩緩暈開，比起她昂首露出優美頸子高唱的歌曲更加無依、也更加堅毅。在同名作品〈薇奧菈在草地嬉戲〉中，我讀到那種不應當被任何「大人」責難的真心（innocence）：無所事事地面對

024

所有事，永遠——為什麼不？這種清爽純粹的質素，宿命地無可避免地在所有人抽長身子的過程中逸散掉了。我們都曾經是一本字典，初版的內頁沒有收錄「計畫」、「報償」這類詞彙，對渾然不知是否會到來的明天，抱持憧憬和焦慮，是多麼浪費的事啊。

試想，一個七歲的小女孩，有什麼理由必須思考自己降生到這世界上的意義呢？她只需要握住掌中的蒲公英（也可以吹散，只要她想）、練習在綠油油的草地上倒立、縱聲大笑，只因為她當下無比快樂。在拉娜‧德芮的筆下，那小女孩名叫薇奧菈，她隨時可以離開任何派對。

〈LA，我哪有資格愛你？〉是我私心最迷戀的一首。

「我」作為一個愛的囚徒，一而再、再而三地呼喚洛杉磯這座城市的名字，同時嘗試奪回她（或許因為登上舞台而失去）的話語權：「我」並不是那麼派

025

對動物，不如外界揣測的服膺於浮華感官；「我」懂得愛也敢愛，同時完全明白「不被愛」的沉默何其苦澀：「**他們說我爲錢而來＼但我沒有＼我甚至沒有愛人＼這不公平**」。

自由的反面，卽是名爲「愛」的綑綁衣——愛過的人，都明白這個鋪天蓋地的道理。然而，在〈離開你之後的事〉裡，拉娜・德芮嘗試找到新的解法：一個人，首先必須是「一個人」，接著才有可能成爲女人、妻子、女友、情人、母親、好友：「**此刻一切已完美＼我有本錢能虛度＼幾朵完美花瓣＼幾張綠色刺繡椅＼等我挑件夏日洋裝**」。

她自陳這本書裡面的字句，有些一開始便是完整的型態了。其餘一些靈光，則是以碎片的型態出現，由她反覆琢磨、拼湊以賦予魂魄——前提是，她讓它們

026

誠實地做本來的樣子。於是，讀者或許可以發現，她的詩句裡頭總有些三關鍵詞反覆被強調。這或許代表了創作者的執迷，也是她仰賴直覺寫字的證據。

她難道不是二十一世紀的瑪格莉特・莒哈絲（Marguerite Duras），在紐約呼喊著她LA的名字？她是這樣的一個人，你的目光無可救藥地順從她的背影遠去。你望著她昂首挺胸地走，往狂暴粗野的地方前進。你親眼看見她的身形越變越小，最終以無憂的孩童型態消失在荒野中。然後，你發現自己遺落已久的耳朵，不知何時已經回到你的身上。

在充滿險惡暗礁的大人生活中，我們沒有理由拒絕拉娜・德芮的邀約，暫時拆掉內嵌的世故與矜持，帶上顏色最大膽的野餐巾和幾瓶嗆到不行的氣泡水，去參加一場隨時可以離席的草地派對。

風格即詩意：讀拉娜‧德芮《薇奧菈在草地嬉戲》

盛浩偉

穿透毛玻璃而霧成一團的午後日光。光暈裡緩緩飄動的微塵。成堆的靜靜積在陰影裡的二手書。書裡紙頁沾滿時間的氣味。老舊的冷氣機轟隆隆運轉著。曾經有一段時間，我常和A待在他的房間裡。我們會躺在床上，各自做著各自的事，翻閱看過幾遍了的小說，滑滑手機，好像有大片大片的時光可以打發，但其實並沒有看上去那麼悠閒。

當時我們各自有各自的困境，我們彼此也幾乎要成為彼此的困境。

如果人與人之間的關係是一條繩子，那麼連結著我和A之間的繩子已經瀕臨斷裂，只靠著剩下的寥寥幾絲纖維撐著；但這寥寥幾絲纖維卻比想像得還堅韌，度過了好多次爭吵。總之是在那樣一段時間，那樣一種狀態中，在A的房間裡，背景總是播放著拉娜・德芮（Lana Del Rey）。

事後回想，這簡直就是某人拍攝的電影，選了一段如此適合的配樂。拉娜・德芮的歌，就是訴說這樣的故事。不是哪一首歌，而是每一首歌。那背後的核

031

心，都是這樣的故事。慵懶，微厭世，淡淡哀愁，必然的遺憾。並不轟轟烈烈，沒有山盟海誓，可情感卻像那樣低語呢喃的歌聲，綿綿密密地沁入骨髓。愛，與愛不得。啊但是，不，也許並不是我印象中這樣地篤定。也許只是因為我太記得那段與A共處的時間，以致於將那時所有的感受全投射到拉娜·德芮的歌曲上；以致於，我個人的記憶，我對A的記憶，與她的音樂牢牢綑綁在一起了。畢竟，那是多麼適合投射這種感受的音樂呢。可能我只是粗略瞥過幾句歌詞，草率地抓住那些與當下狀態相仿的片段。

而如今讀她的詩集，《薇奧菈在草地嬉戲》，才有機會忽略音樂，忽略那迷幻的旋律與配樂，單純專注在字詞上。而我彷彿可以肯定當時的記憶與感受。比如讀到〈手機鈴聲〉：「**我真的好喜歡你／你一沒打來我就緊張兮兮／我順著呼吸隔空對你／說別訓練我的堅毅／我真的只想脆弱溫柔／若你能讓我做我自己／你將是我生命中的唯一**」——其實濃烈，卻深藏在心；想要就此不在意，卻反倒

更加在意。確實，是這樣一種猶豫不決、將明未明的心情。

又如〈開心〉，詩句與題名形成強烈張力。詩末的句子寫道：「想到你最後一次躺在我身邊／尖峰時的車聲越來越大，越來越大／成了一條小河或激流／我倆好似在水中優遊／而這不只是一場夢／我們是真的很／／開心」——失去之後，想起什麼都覺得是好的。但是當初為什麼會選擇結束呢？又或者，我們只是習慣竄改自己的記憶罷了。為了讓自己好過一點。為了讓自己好過一點。

詩裡的「我」原本思慮周密，謹慎斟酌，但就在遂行內心決定之時：「看見了薇奧菈／在草地上嬉戲／七歲的她手裡／緊抓著蒲公英／倒立弓身像座橋／如狂人般咧嘴笑／滿溢無所事事才能迸發的活力／等待著煙火綻放的絢麗／／就在那一瞬間／我決定無所事事地面對所有事」。這是典型的神悟（epiphany）時刻，是所有世故與算計、所有對未來的憂慮，都被童稚天真給化解的瞬間。愛情

這是詩集同名作〈薇奧菈在草地嬉戲〉的核心動機。

033

令人煩躁，令人處處計較，令人痛。但有沒有可能，會痛的並不是愛？會不會像是另一首詩〈離開你之後的事〉裡寫到的：在離開之後，才真正感受到「**此刻一切已完美／我有本錢能虛度**」。

離開A的時候，老實說，也曾閃過這樣的感受。但隨後則是惆悵。

我們的問題，靠著結束一段關係而解決，這是否意味著這段關係本身就是問題的根源？然而當初的情感卻是如此地真實而具體，具體如這些詩句，以鉛字銘刻記憶。記憶陳放在那個午後的沒有開燈的房間裡，轟轟作響的老舊冷氣伴隨著拉娜・德芮的低語旋律。這種風格也許就是詩意的所在，失意的所在。當下的難受。事過境遷的美好。為什麼最後會離開呢？也許是因為，我和A都已經各自看見屬於自己的薇奧菈了。但願如此。

著火的屋子與忘記逃跑的人

潘柏霖

自我著迷與自我毀滅或許一直是Lana Del Rey的品牌形象。

從她的歌曲〈Born To Die〉中那句：「有時候愛根本沒有用，路程崎嶇，我做的所有事情都是為了你。」，到〈Video Games〉中的「是你，就是你，我會等你一百年」、〈This Is What Make Us Girls〉的「我們女孩就是這樣，我們不團結」，到〈Blue Jeans〉中的「我會愛你直到世界末日，我會等你一百年」、〈Cinnamon Girl〉中的「如果你擁抱我沒有傷害我，我們為愛爭破頭」，都不斷讓我想像到一個把長髮瀏海吹得很高的女人（或者男人或者其他性別都可以啦，我不在乎），躺在靠海的小屋前方的躺椅上，沒有哭，但看起來非常悲傷。如果要說得美好一點，Lana的歌詞風格或許可以說是復古沉醉，說直接一點其實就是無病呻吟，這當然是多少都會受到批評，畢竟沒有人想要看一個有錢優越的人躺在那邊說自己生活很痛苦——但為什麼不？怎樣的病才是值得喊痛的？怎樣的痛苦才算是真的痛苦？優越的人所受到

037

的苦難道就不是苦難嗎？在我沒有這麼痛恨資本主義小蜥蜴的時候，我會這樣捍衛自己（那個喜歡聽Lana歌的我自己），在我比較痛恨自己的時候，我會覺得自己就像是那個躺在躺椅上面明明沒發生任何真正系統性毀滅的災難，卻還是站不起來的垃圾。

或許我也是這樣看待Lana Del Rey的？

Lana Del Rey出版的詩集《薇奧菈在草地上嬉戲》除了紙本與電子書外，原文還有有聲書版本，是由Lana自己朗讀，背景由Jack Antonoff配樂，而Jack也是Lana Del Rey上一張專輯《Norman Fucking Rockwell!》的製作人之一。如果希望能夠在詩集中找到和Lana歌曲中相似感受的話，或許你會喜歡這本詩集，但除此之外其實也別無他物——大多數的詩作都擁有相似於她歌曲中那種懶散靡爛的恍惚嗑藥感，而沒有這部分的詩作則稍嫌無聊沒有特色，總括來說，她最迷人的地方，不在於她試圖解釋自己所處的現實世界，不在於形容現

實世界是什麼，而在於她試圖向讀者解釋自己，剖開自己的肉，打開拉鍊，讓所有人看看她的裡面──就算好像是很空的，那也一樣精彩。

這狀況很明確顯示在她這本詩集中我認為最好的兩首詩裡，與詩集同名的這首詩〈薇奧菈在草地嬉戲〉，定調了整本詩主要的走向，在這首詩中，敍事者

「我」決定，要「無所事事地面對所有事情」。

「我」進了門後，卻看見了七歲的「薇奧菈」在草地上嬉戲，而那個畫面讓

「我」去了派對，思前想後，盤算究竟等等該做些什麼來面對大家，但在

「我」的侷促不安，使得「我」放下掙扎，不再計較是否該努力做任何事情，

情，薇奧菈在草地上嬉戲象徵了某種清純童稚，簡單自然的快樂感，對應到先前

在這首詩裡，可以看出Lana一貫的自我檢視頓悟，那是非常非常微小的事

以不變應萬變。看上去是糜爛退守，實際上則是攤開雙手接納一切可能性。這裡

Lana的自我理解，很有效果地傳達給觀眾（以免你不懂，觀眾是我）。

而在〈開心〉這首詩中，開頭一句「你以爲我很富有 的確 但不是你想的那樣」就定調了整首詩的節奏以及想要傳遞的內容，這首詩就是在反應自己被大眾誤解的狀況，試圖提出一個解釋，其實內容是很簡單的，大意上就是在說你們以爲我很有錢，但不是，我是心靈富有。這種內容雖然放在一個知名歌手身上，稍嫌假掰，但誠如我開頭所說，自我著迷一直都是Lana Del Rey的品牌形象，她寫得最動人的歌詞，最美的詩，都是她在自我著迷，以及著迷到想要被愛毀滅（通常是被愛毀滅）的過程狀態──我思考了很久，要怎樣替這本詩集找到適合的受衆，很久很久我想到了這個形容（絕對不是因爲截稿日要到了）──想像一個畫面，有一個人（不管性別種族隨你選），坐在一座屋子的門口前很遠，門外有一座湖，湖裡面很顯然有怪物，怪物伸出觸手在湖邊左搖右晃，好幾次幾乎都要掃到那個人的腳了，很可能就會把那個人直接拉進湖底。而忽然那個人背後的屋

040

子著火了，火勢大開，整間屋子都被火焰給吞食，而那個人，對，你記得那個你選了的人嗎？他一樣繼續坐在那屋子前面，你以為他會跑走，你以為他會害怕，但沒有，他就是坐在那間著火的屋子前面，一樣待在那有怪物的湖的前面，就只是看著那些東西。

如果你覺得那個畫面很漂亮。

如果你喜歡那樣的畫面，或許你會喜歡這本詩集。

在沒有明天的狂亂中漫舞

作　　　者／HUSH、鄭宜農、徐珮芬、盛浩偉、潘柏霖
榮譽發行人／黃鎮隆
總　經　理／陳君平
協　經　理／洪琇菁
總　編　輯／呂尚燁
主　　　編／劉銘廷
美術總監／沙雲佩
美術編輯／李政儀
行銷宣傳／楊玉如、洪國瑋
國際版權／黃令歡、梁名儀
內文排版／尚騰印刷事業有限公司

出　　　版／城邦文化事業股份有限公司　尖端出版
　　　　　　台北市中山區民生東路二段一四一號十樓
　　　　　　電話：（○二）二五○○—七六○○
　　　　　　傳真：（○二）二五○○—二六八三

　　　　　　E-mail：7novels@mail2.spp.com.tw

發　　　行／英屬蓋曼群島商家庭傳媒股份有限公司城邦分公司　尖端出版
　　　　　　台北市中山區民生東路二段一四一號十樓
　　　　　　電話：（○二）二五○○—七六○○（代表號）
　　　　　　傳真：（○二）二五○○—一九七九

法律顧問／王子文律師　元禾法律事務所
　　　　　　台北市羅斯福路三段三十七號十五樓

二○二三年三月一版一刷